BIG BUSHY MUSTACHE

PIC
SOT

by Gary Soto

illustrated by
Joe Cepeda

Alfred A. Knopf  New York

para José Padilla
and his big bushy mustache

&

Deborah Escobedo
and her big beautiful hairdo
—G. S.

For our beautiful son, Julian Matías,
"*Pingo* wild baby of the West"
—J. C.

THIS IS A BORZOI BOOK PUBLISHED BY ALFRED A. KNOPF, INC.

Text copyright © 1998 by Gary Soto
Illustrations copyright © 1998 by Joe Cepeda
All rights reserved under International and Pan-American Copyright Conventions. Published in
the United States of America by Alfred A. Knopf, Inc., New York, and simultaneously in Canada
by Random House of Canada Limited, Toronto. Distributed by Random House, Inc., New York.

http://www.randomhouse.com/

Library of Congress Cataloging-in-Publication Data
Soto, Gary.
Big bushy mustache / by Gary Soto ; illustrations by Joe Cepeda.
p.   cm.
Summary: In order to look more like his father, Ricky borrows a mustache from
a school costume, but when he loses it on the way home his father comes up
with a replacement.
ISBN 0-679-88030-5 (trade) — ISBN 0-679-98030-X (lib. bdg.)
[1. Mustache—Fiction. 2. Fathers and sons—Fiction.
3. Mexican Americans—Fiction.] I. Cepeda, Joe, ill. II. Title.
PZ7.S7242Bi   1998
[E]—dc20   97-18211

Printed in the United States of America
10 9 8 7 6 5 4 3 2 1

$\mathcal{P}$eople always said Ricky looked just like his mother.

"He has beautiful eyes, exactly like yours, Rosa!" said Mrs. Sanchez, the crossing guard, as his mother took him to school one morning.

"Thanks!" Ricky's mother shouted, and turned a big smile on him. "Have a good day, *mi'jo*." Then she gave him a kiss.

Ricky went into school frowning. He was a boy. Why didn't people say he looked like his father?

That morning his teacher, Mrs. Cortez, brought out a large box from the closet and set it on her desk. She took out a hat and a *sarape*. She took out a sword and raised it toward the ceiling.

"Class, for our next unit we're going to do a play about *Cinco de Mayo*. That's a holiday that celebrates the Mexican victory over the French army."

Mrs. Cortez looked around the room. Her eyes settled on Ricky. "Ricky, do you want to carry the sword?"

Ricky shook his head no.

"Do you want to wear this white shirt?" she asked.

Again Ricky shook his head no. And he shook his head to the
sombrero, the captain's hat, the toy pistol and holster, the purple
cape, the tiny Mexican flag.

But when Mrs. Cortez took out a big, bushy mustache, something clicked. This time Ricky nodded yes.

For the rest of the day, the class practiced their parts. Some of the children played Mexican soldiers. Some of the children played French soldiers.

All the while, Ricky played with his mustache. It tickled his lip. It made him feel tough.

When school was over, Mrs. Cortez told the class to leave the costumes in their desks.

Ricky took off his mustache. But instead of leaving it behind, he put it in his pocket. He wanted to take it home. He wanted to surprise his father when he got home from work.

Maybe Mami will take a picture of us, he thought. *We could stand next to each other in front of our new car.*

After Ricky left the school, he pressed the mustache back
onto his lip. He felt grown-up.

A man on the street called out, "Hello, soldier."

Ricky passed a woman carrying groceries. She said, "What a handsome young man."

He passed a kindergartner, who said, "Mister, would you help me tie my shoes?"

Ricky laughed and ran home. He climbed the wooden steps, pushed open the door, and rushed into the kitchen, where his mother was peeling apples.

"*¡Hola, Mami!*" he said. "I'm hungry."

He looked up and waited for her to say something about his big, bushy mustache.

But she only smiled and handed him a slice of apple.

"*Mi'jo*, wash your hands and help me with the apples," she said.

Ricky's smile disappeared. Didn't she notice?

"Look, Mami. Isn't my *bigote* great?" he said, tugging at her apron.

His mother looked at him.

"*¿Bigote?* What are you talking about?"

"This one," he said. He touched his lip, but the mustache was gone! He felt around his face. It was not on his cheek. It was not on his chin. He looked down to the floor, but it wasn't there, either.

I must have lost it on the way home, Ricky thought. Without saying anything, he ran out the front door.

He retraced his steps, eyes wide open. He dug through a pile of raked leaves. He parted the tall grass that grew along a fence. He looked in the street, between parked cars, and in flower beds.

He jumped with hope when he saw a black thing. But when he bent
over to pick it up, he discovered that it was a squashed crayon.
Ricky sat on the curb and cried. The mustache was gone.

When he got home, Ricky told his mother what had happened.
She wiped her hands on a dish towel and hugged him.

At dinner, he wanted to tell Papi too, but the words would not come out. They were stuck in his throat.

He watched his father's big, bushy mustache move up and down when he chewed.

Under his breath, Ricky whispered, "Mustache," but his father didn't hear. He talked about his work.

After dinner, Ricky went to his bedroom. With a black crayon, he colored a sheet of paper and then cut it into the shape of a mustache. He taped it to his mouth and stood before the mirror. But it didn't look real. He tore it off, crumpled it, and tossed it on the floor.

In the closet, Ricky found a can of black shoe polish. He looked in the mirror and smeared a line above his lip, but it was too flat, not thick and bushy at all.

Finally, he dug out a pair of old shoes. The strings were black. He cut them in short strips and bound them together with a rubber band. He held the creation above his lip. It looked like a black mop. And smelled like old socks.

That night, after he put on his pajamas, Ricky went into the
living room, where his father was listening to the radio.

"Papi, I lost my mustache . . . *mi bigote*."

His father laughed. "What mustache?"

Ricky climbed into his father's lap and told him everything. His father smiled and told him a story about a hen that tried to become a swan. It was a good story, but it still didn't solve his problem. Tomorrow he would have to face Mrs. Cortez.

The next morning, Ricky got out of bed slowly. He dressed slowly. He combed his hair slowly. At breakfast, he chewed his cereal slowly. He raised his eyes slowly when his father came into the kitchen. *"Buenos días,"* he greeted Ricky.

Then Ricky's mother came into the kitchen. "*Mi'jo*, I have a
surprise for you," she said.

Mami held out a closed fist and let it open like a flower. Sitting in her
palm was a mustache. It was big and bushy.

"You found it!" Ricky shouted happily.

"Well, yes and no," Mami said as she poured herself a cup of coffee.

Ricky pressed the new mustache to his lip.
He ate his cereal, and the mustache moved up and
down, just like his father's.

But something was different about his father's smile. His lip looked
funny. Ricky jumped up and threw his arms around Papi's neck.

"*Gracias*, Papi! Thank you!" he cried.

"That's okay," Papi told him. "But next time listen to your teacher."

Then Papi touched his son's hair softly. "And, hey, now I look just like you!"

Ricky grinned a mile wide.

When Ricky walked to school, he carried the
mustache not on his lip, but safely in his pocket.

It wasn't just a bushy disguise anymore, but a
gift from his papi.